## The Boxcar Children Mysteries

The Mystery of the Secret Message

The Firehouse Mystery

The Mystery in San Francisco

The Niagara Falls Mystery

The Mystery at the Alamo

The Outer Space Mystery

The Soccer Mystery

The Mystery in the Old Attic

The Growling Bear Mystery

The Mystery of the Lake Monster

The Mystery at Peacock Hall

The Windy City Mystery

The Black Pearl Mystery

The Cereal Box Mystery

The Panther Mystery

The Mystery of the Queen's Jewels

The Stolen Sword Mystery

The Basketball Mystery

The Movie Star Mystery

The Mystery of the Pirate's Map

The Ghost Town Mystery

The Mystery of the Black Raven

The Mystery in the Mall

The Mystery in New York

The Gymnastics Mystery

The Poison Frog Mystery

The Mystery of the Empty Safe

The Home Run Mystery

The Great Bicycle Race Mystery

The Mystery of the Wild Ponies

The Mystery in the Computer Game

The Mystery at the Crooked House

The Hockey Mystery

The Mystery of the Midnight Dog

The Mystery of the Screech Owl

The Summer Camp Mystery

The Copycat Mystery

The Haunted Clock Tower Mystery

The Mystery of the Tiger's Eye

The Disappearing Staircase Mystery

The Mystery on Blizzard Mountain

The Mystery of the Spider's Clue

The Candy Factory Mystery

The Mystery of the Mummy's Curse

The Mystery of the Star Ruby

The Stuffed Bear Mystery

The Mystery of Alligator Swamp

The Mystery at Skeleton Point

The Tattletale Mystery

The Comic Book Mystery

The Great Shark Mystery

The Ice Cream Mystery

The Midnight Mystery

The Mystery in the Fortune Cookie

The Black Widow Spider Mystery

The Radio Mystery

The Mystery of the Runaway Ghost

The Finders Keepers Mystery

The Mystery of the Haunted Boxcar

# THE MYSTERY OF THE HAUNTED BOXCAR

created by
## GERTRUDE CHANDLER WARNER

*Illustrated by Hodges Soileau*

ALBERT WHITMAN & Company
Morton Grove, Illinois

ISBN 0-8075-5554-1

1 3 5 7 9 10 8 6 4 2

Printed in the U.S.A.

# Contents

CHAPTER 1

# A Haunted Boxcar

"Watch your back!" Benny Alden called to his sister Violet, who was dribbling a soccer ball across their front yard. Their older brother, Henry, was hot on her trail, trying to get the ball.

Violet quickly passed the ball to Benny. Their sister, Jessie, lunged at Benny to steal the ball away. But just in time, Benny shot the ball between the two cones set up at the edge of the yard.

"Goal!" Benny cried.

"Nice play!" Violet said, giving Benny

a high five. They were both grinning proudly. Even though Violet was ten years old and Benny only six, they'd just won the soccer game against twelve-year-old Jessie and fourteen-year-old Henry.

"Good job!" their grandfather, James Alden, called from the other side of the yard where he'd been playing goalie for Violet and Benny's team.

Jessie collapsed in a heap on the grass, out of breath. "Good game, you guys."

Watch, the family dog, ran over to Jessie and began licking her face. "Hey, Watch," Jessie said. "We needed you on our team."

"He could have been our goalie," suggested Henry with a laugh. He plopped down beside Jessie.

The Aldens were all sitting on the grass, catching their breath, when they heard a voice calling from the edge of the yard. "Hello!"

They looked over to see their neighbor, Florence Murray, walking toward them. She was a small woman with bright blue eyes and white hair. With her were a bearded man and a young girl whom the Aldens didn't recognize. The man was wearing a tweed jacket. The girl had big brown eyes and blond hair pulled up in a ponytail. She looked a little younger than Violet.

"Hello," the Aldens called back as they all got to their feet. Watch ran to greet the visitors.

"I want to introduce my brother and my niece," Ms. Murray said. "This is Arthur and his daughter, Claire. They'll be staying with me for a little while. These are the Aldens, whom I was telling you about."

"Nice to meet you," Mr. Alden said, shaking Arthur Murray's hand.

"Welcome to Greenfield," said Henry.

Watch barked and everyone laughed. "I guess Watch is saying 'welcome,' too!" said Jessie.

"My brother is a history professor. He's staying with me while he does some research at the Greenfield library," Ms. Murray explained.

"We saw you playing soccer," said Professor Murray. "Claire loves to play soccer. Don't you, honey?"

Claire ducked her head and turned away shyly.

"You should join us," said Violet. "My team could use another player."

Jessie laughed. "*We're* the ones who need another player!"

Claire gave a timid smile, but she remained partly hidden behind her father.

"What sort of research are you doing, Arthur?" Mr. Alden asked.

"I'm writing a book on the railroad and how it has affected our country's history," Professor Murray said.

"We've got a piece of railroad history right here in our yard," said Henry.

"You do?" Professor Murray said, raising his eyebrows.

"Wait till you see!" cried Benny, running around the house to the backyard. Watch chased after him. "Follow me!" Benny shouted.

Professor Murray stopped in his tracks when he saw where Benny was leading them. "Is that a real antique boxcar?" he asked, staring in disbelief at the bright red train car nestled among the trees at the back of the Aldens' yard.

"It sure is," said Jessie. "Come and see."

Professor Murray walked quickly across the yard. When he reached the boxcar, he placed his hand gently on the outside and ran his hand along the wooden panels. He turned to the Aldens. "Where did you find it? How did it end up *here*?"

The Aldens looked at one another and grinned. "It's kind of a long story," Jessie began. "You see, our parents died, and we were supposed to go live with our grandfather." She smiled at Mr. Alden.

"But we didn't know him," said Violet, "and we were afraid he wasn't nice."

"So we ran away!" Benny added.

Now Henry took up the story. "We found this old boxcar in the woods and made it our home."

"But when we finally met Grandfather, we realized he wasn't mean after all," Violet said. "So we came to live with him here in Greenfield."

"And Grandfather had the boxcar moved to the backyard for us!" said Benny.

"And they've been a happy family ever since," said Ms. Murray.

Benny jumped up onto the stump that was the boxcar's front step. "Come on in!" He rolled the door open and stepped inside, motioning for the others to join him.

Professor Murray and Claire stepped carefully into the boxcar. Henry, Violet, and Jessie followed. Grandfather and Ms. Murray remained outside, throwing a ball to Watch.

Professor Murray took a deep breath and looked around slowly. "This is amazing. I feel I've stepped back in time."

The Aldens smiled proudly. They loved their boxcar and were pleased to share it.

Professor Murray walked around, gently touching the wooden walls, the ceiling, even squatting down to look at the floor.

"Would you like to sit down?" Jessie asked, pulling out a chair for him.

The professor looked surprised. Apparently he had been so intent on studying the boxcar that he hadn't noticed the table and chairs inside. "What's all this for?" he asked.

"The boxcar is our playhouse!" Benny said.

"Your playhouse?" Claire repeated, her eyes lighting up. It was the first thing the Aldens had heard her say.

"We like to play here and — " Jessie began, but Professor Murray interrupted her.

"Your *playhouse*?" he asked sharply. "You *play* in here?"

"Yes," said Benny. "It's really fun."

Professor Murray looked upset. "This boxcar is a treasure from the past, a valuable antique. It should be in a museum, where it could be taken care of properly. There shouldn't be children playing in it."

"But we love our boxcar," Benny said quietly.

"We take good care of it," Jessie added. "We clean it and make sure all the boards are in good shape."

"We've even repainted it when the paint was peeling," said Henry.

Professor Murray frowned but did not argue. Then he looked at his watch and sighed. "I wish I could stay to look around some more, but I have an appointment I can't miss." He stepped reluctantly out of the boxcar. "Come on, Claire."

Claire looked sad to leave the boxcar, too. As the others were talking, she'd been walking around, looking at the books and games the Aldens kept there.

Claire turned to Violet and opened her mouth as if she were about to ask her something. But then she seemed to change her mind. "Good-bye," she said softly, before following her father out.

Professor Murray turned around and took one more look at the boxcar. Suddenly, a strange look came over his face.

"What is it, Dad?" Claire asked.

"Oh, nothing," he said. "I was just thinking . . ." His words trailed off. When he spoke again, his voice sounded mysterious. "I was just thinking about all the history a train car like this carries. All the people who worked or rode on this boxcar — each of them left a little bit of themselves behind."

Professor Murray shook his head slightly,

then smiled down at Claire and took her hand. They walked briskly over to where Ms. Murray was saying good-bye to Grandfather.

"Wow," said Jessie, as she watched them go. "Professor Murray really didn't like it that we use the boxcar as our playhouse."

"No, he didn't," Henry agreed.

"I wish Claire could have stayed and played," said Violet. "She seemed lonely."

Henry nodded. "And shy."

Jessie looked thoughtful. "It was interesting what Professor Murray said, though, about the history of our boxcar and all the people who have used it. I never thought about that before."

Benny turned to her, his face aglow. "He said everyone who's been in our boxcar left a bit of themselves behind. Do you think he's talking about ghosts? It sounded like he thinks our boxcar is *haunted*."

The others laughed.

"Oh, Benny," said Jessie. "You know there's no such thing as a ghost."

But Benny didn't look so sure.

CHAPTER 2

## A Light in the Night

The next morning when the Alden children woke up, they smelled something delicious from the kitchen. They dressed quickly and ran downstairs. Mrs. McGregor, their housekeeper, was making scrambled eggs and sausage.

"That smells great!" said Henry, taking a stack of plates from the cabinet. As he began setting the table, Jessie and Violet got glasses and poured orange juice. Benny put out forks and napkins.

"Looks like a beautiful day," Mrs.

McGregor said, bringing the steaming plate of eggs to the table.

"It sure does," Grandfather agreed, joining them. Sunlight streamed in the window and the sky was bright blue.

Breakfast tasted as good as it smelled. As the children ate, they talked about what they would do that day. They were just putting their dishes in the sink when the doorbell rang. Watch ran barking to the front hall.

"Who could that be so early?" Mrs. McGregor said.

"I'll go see!" Benny cried, hurrying to the door.

When Benny pulled open the front door, he was surprised to see Professor Murray and Claire. With them was a woman he'd never seen before. She was tall, with freckles and curly reddish-brown hair.

"Hello!" Benny said in his friendly way.

"Good morning," said Professor Murray. Claire smiled shyly.

The other Aldens joined Benny at the front door.

"Won't you come in?" Grandfather asked.

"Thank you," Professor Murray said, stepping into the front hall. He motioned to the woman beside him. "Please allow me to introduce Amelia, a fellow railroad fan. We met at the library and I mentioned your boxcar."

Amelia smiled and jumped in. "I just had to see it. I hope you don't mind that I came."

"Not at all," said Henry.

"We'd love to show you our boxcar," Jessie added.

"Thank you," Professor Murray said.

"Yes, thanks," Amelia added.

"Please excuse me for not joining you," Grandfather said. "I need to finish packing for my business trip."

As they walked out of the house, Violet noticed a purple car parked at the curb in front of their house. She nudged Claire. "Is that Amelia's car?"

"Yes," Claire replied.

"Wow — nice color," Violet said softly. Purple was her favorite.

Claire smiled.

Once again, Benny led the way to the backyard, with Watch at his heels.

As the boxcar came into view, Amelia's face lit up. "It's just like I imagined!" she said.

"May we go in?" Professor Murray asked, stepping up on the stump in front of the door.

"Of course," said Jessie.

Professor Murray rolled open the door, and Amelia followed him inside. The children stayed outside with Watch.

"I have a dog at home," Claire said, stroking Watch's furry back. "Her name's Charlotte. We couldn't bring her with us, though — my Aunt Flo's allergic."

"You can come play with Watch whenever you're missing Charlotte," Benny said.

"Thanks. I'd like that," said Claire.

Amelia stepped out of the boxcar, a big smile on her face. "This is truly a special place," she said.

"Are you a train professor, too?" Benny asked.

"Me? Oh, no," Amelia laughed. "No, I . . . well, I just like old trains. That's all." She laughed again, but this time it sounded a little forced. "So has the boxcar always been here?" she asked.

"No, our grandfather moved it to the backyard for us when we came to live with him," Henry explained. "But we found it not so far from here."

"Really?" Amelia asked, sounding quite interested. "In Silver City?"

Jessie's eyebrows shot up in surprise. "Actually, yes," she said. "How did you know that?"

"Oh, just a lucky guess," Amelia said. "Is it true that you used to *live* in it?"

"I know that sounds strange," Jessie said, nodding.

Amelia smiled mysteriously. "I've heard stranger stories." She ran her hand over the outside of the boxcar. Her face had a distant look, as if she was deep in thought.

"Is something wrong?" Benny asked.

Benny's question seemed to shake Amelia out of her thoughts. "No, nothing's wrong.

I was just trying to picture a family living in here."

"It was a good home," Jessie said.

Just then, Professor Murray emerged from the boxcar. "Thanks for letting us see this again," he said. "I do wish you'd consider giving it to a museum. They could put it on display and make sure it isn't damaged. Talk it over with your grandfather, will you?"

The Aldens were stunned. They didn't think they could ever give their boxcar away. But they didn't want to be rude, so Jessie said, "We'll think about it."

Professor Murray gave a satisfied nod. "Well, come along, Claire," he called as he and Amelia walked away.

Claire looked up from patting Watch. Watch was wagging his tail, enjoying all the attention. Claire gave him one last pat, then stood up reluctantly and ran to catch up with her father.

When the Aldens returned to the house, Grandfather was coming down the stairs with a large suitcase. He was leaving soon for a business trip.

"Do you have to go away already?" Benny asked.

"Don't worry, Benny," Grandfather said. "I'll be back before you know it. While I'm gone, I know you'll all help Mrs. McGregor take care of things."

"Of course we will," Jessie said.

"Did Professor Murray's friend like the boxcar?" Grandfather asked.

"Yes . . . but Professor Murray wants us to give our boxcar away," said Benny, setting his face in a frown.

"He does?" Mr. Alden said, surprised. "To whom?"

"To a museum. He said it's too valuable for kids to use as a playhouse," Jessie explained.

"Hmm," said Grandfather. "I'm sure the boxcar *is* valuable — but you four take good care of it, and I know it means a lot to you. I'm sure it's perfectly safe here."

The children smiled. They'd known Grandfather would understand.

Mr. Alden checked his watch. "I'd better get going or I'll miss my flight." He set down his suitcase and gave each of the children a hug.

"We'll miss you," Violet said.

"Yeah, who will be our goalie?" asked Benny.

"Try Mrs. McGregor," said Mr. Alden over his shoulder as he headed out to the garage.

The children smiled. Somehow they couldn't quite picture Mrs. McGregor out in the yard playing soccer.

The children spent the afternoon in the boxcar playing board games. When Mrs. McGregor called them in for dinner, they put the games away neatly and tucked the chairs under the table.

As they stepped out of the boxcar, Benny felt some raindrops on his face. "It's starting to rain," he said. "Make sure the door is shut tightly."

Violet slid the door shut and gave it a pat. Then they all ran to the house to eat.

It rained all through dinner, and while

the Aldens washed the dishes, and when they were getting ready for bed, too. It was still raining when Jessie read Benny two chapters in his book before tucking him into bed. The book was a mystery story, Benny's favorite kind. Jessie and Benny talked about the suspects in the book and who the bad guy might be.

"Maybe it's the man who lives next door," Benny said.

"Could be," said Jessie mysteriously. "Or maybe not — you'll have to wait and see." Jessie had read the book when she was Benny's age, and she remembered the ending. "We'll read more tomorrow. Now it's bedtime."

"Just one more chapter?" Benny begged.

"No. It's definitely time for bed." Jessie's voice was firm.

"All right," said Benny, snuggling down under his covers.

Jessie smoothed Benny's blanket and turned off the light. "Good night," she called, closing his door behind her.

Benny lay on his side, listening to the

rain falling outside. He thought about his book and wondered whether the man next door really was the bad guy. He thought about all the characters, wishing Jessie had read just a little bit more. He wondered what would happen in the next chapter.

Benny shifted onto his other side and thought about Professor Murray and what he had said about the boxcar. Did Professor Murray really think the boxcar was haunted? Was that why he didn't think the Aldens should play in it?

Just then, Benny heard a noise outside. He sat up in bed. What was that? He went quickly to the window and looked out. The backyard was dark. But then Benny spotted something that made him gasp.

"I don't believe it!" he said out loud. "The boxcar really *is* haunted!"

CHAPTER 3

# A Break-In

Benny burst out of his room and ran into the room next door. "Henry! Henry!" he cried.

Henry was lying in bed, reading a book. He looked up, surprised. "Benny? What is it? Did you have a bad dream?"

Benny grabbed Henry's arm. "Come look! Professor Murray was right!" He tried to pull Henry to his feet.

Henry put down the book and struggled to stop Benny from yanking on his arm. "All right, all right! Hang on!" Henry stood up.

"Professor Murray was right about what?"

"The boxcar!" Benny said. "It's haunted. I saw a light." He pulled Henry over to the window and lifted the shade. "Look!"

Henry looked out, and so did Benny. There was nothing there.

"But — " Benny sputtered. "There was a light out there a minute ago. Keep watching. I'm sure it will come back."

The two boys looked out the window for several minutes. "What exactly did you see before?" Henry asked.

"There was a light near the boxcar," Benny said. "It was kind of floating around."

"Are you sure it wasn't just a dream?" Henry asked, yawning.

"No, it wasn't a dream!" Benny said. He looked out the window again, but the yard was completely dark.

"Maybe it was lightning," Henry suggested.

"It didn't look like lightning," Benny said. "It floated around, like a ghost."

Just then the door opened and Jessie and

Violet came in, dressed in their pajamas and looking sleepy. "What's going on?" Jessie asked.

"Benny thought he saw a light out near the boxcar," Henry said.

Jessie and Violet went to the window to look. The yard was still dark.

"I *did* see a light, but now it's gone," Benny said.

"Are you sure you didn't just dream this?" asked Jessie.

"That's what I asked," Henry said.

"No, I didn't dream it. It was *real*," said Benny.

"Well, there's only one thing to do," Jessie said.

The others looked at her expectantly. Benny was afraid she'd say that the only thing to do was go back to bed.

But instead she said, "Let's go take a look."

"*Now?*" Benny asked, his eyes widening. "In the dark? In the rain?"

"You're not going to be able to sleep if you're wondering about that light," said Jessie.

The Aldens went downstairs to the back hall. Jessie opened the closet and handed out raincoats. Henry went to the kitchen to get a flashlight.

Watch followed them to the back door. He seemed to be wondering why they were going outside in the middle of the night. He wasn't about to miss any action.

"We have to be quiet," Jessie reminded them. "We don't want to wake up Mrs. McGregor and worry her for no reason."

Henry pushed the door open slowly, and Watch ran out. The backyard was completely dark. It was still raining lightly. "If anyone's out there, Watch will bark. Then we'll head straight back to the house," said Henry.

He turned on the flashlight with a click and shined it out the open door and around the yard. He didn't see anybody or anything out of the ordinary. But somehow the backyard looked unfamiliar and eerie in the glow of the flashlight.

As the Aldens stepped outside, Henry pointed the flashlight in the direction of the boxcar. But the boxcar was too far back in the yard for the beam of light to reach it. All they could see was darkness.

"Come on," said Benny, stepping off the porch and heading across the yard. He was eager to find out what had been making the strange light he'd seen. Jessie and Henry were with him.

Violet walked behind. Now that they were outside, she was beginning to wonder if checking the boxcar was a good idea after all. She reached down and patted Watch's head. She was glad Watch was with them.

The Aldens walked farther into the darkness. "You guys," Violet whispered nervously, "do you think maybe we should go back in? I'm getting wet and — "

But just then the boxcar came into view. And something definitely was not right.

"Did we leave the door open?" Jessie asked.

"No," said Violet. "I closed it before we went inside for dinner."

"Well, it's open now," said Henry. He shined the beam of the flashlight across the

front of the boxcar. Other than the open door, everything looked normal. There was no sign of any ghosts, no light coming from inside, and everything was completely quiet.

"Is anyone there?" called Henry.

There was no answer. The Aldens moved cautiously toward the boxcar. Jessie, Benny, and Henry stepped up into the doorway and peered inside.

"What do you see?" Violet asked.

But they didn't answer. Instead they disappeared inside.

Violet looked back at the house, wishing she'd stayed in bed. But the house was a long, dark backyard away. She stepped up into the boxcar and gasped at what she saw.

One of the chairs was lying on its side, and the neat pile of games had been knocked over onto the floor, spilling pieces everywhere.

There was nobody but the Aldens in the boxcar now.

But someone—or something — had been there that night.

# CHAPTER 4

# The Main Suspects

"Oh my goodness!" said Jessie. "What happened here?"

"A ghost!" Benny cried.

Henry shined the flashlight all around the inside of the boxcar. Aside from the fallen chair and the mess of games, everything else was in its proper place. "These seem to be the only things that were touched. It doesn't look like we were robbed."

"Do you think whoever did this is still around?" asked Violet.

"No," said Henry. "Watch would be

barking if anyone else were in the yard. Right, Watch?"

Watch's ears were up, alert. He was sniffing around curiously, but he stayed silent.

"Can we go back inside the house?" Violet asked, her voice shaky.

"Sure," said Jessie. She picked up the chair that had been knocked over and set it upright. "We'll clean up the games tomorrow, in the light."

The children took one last look around the boxcar and then stepped out. It was still raining. Jessie carefully shut the door, then followed the others back across their yard. Violet felt relieved as their comfortable house appeared in the flashlight's glow.

Once inside, Henry turned off the flashlight. They all removed their wet raincoats.

"How about some hot cocoa?" Jessie offered.

"Good idea," said Benny.

A few minutes later, the Aldens were gathered around the kitchen table with steaming mugs of cocoa in front of them.

"Mmmmm . . . " said Benny as he took

a sip from his mug. A thin layer of chocolate coated his upper lip.

"Do you think we should wake up Mrs. McGregor?" Violet asked.

"And tell her what?" said Henry. "We don't even know what happened."

"Well, we know someone was in there," said Jessie.

"Or some*thing*," said Henry. "It might not have been a person."

"That's just what I was thinking," said Benny. "It might have been a ghost!"

Henry smiled. "That wasn't exactly what I was thinking, Benny. I meant it might have been an animal."

"How would an animal have opened the door?" Violet asked. "I'm sure I shut it before we came in for dinner."

Everyone was silent for a moment.

"Then it must have been a person," Henry said at last.

"But Professor Murray said — " Benny started to protest.

"You know it wasn't a ghost," Jessie said, interrupting.

"I guess not," Benny said, reluctantly. He swirled his cocoa in his cup.

"All right, so we agree it was a person," said Henry. "Who? Why would someone go in our boxcar in the middle of the night?"

"There's nothing valuable to steal," Jessie pointed out.

"Do you think someone was trying to wreck it?" asked Henry.

Jessie thought for a moment before she answered. "I don't think so. I think the mess might have been an accident. Maybe whoever was in there saw the lights go on in the house and got scared. When they ran out of there, they might have just knocked over the chair and games."

Violet yawned. "I don't know about you guys, but I'm ready to go back to bed."

"Me too," said Jessie.

The Aldens rinsed their cocoa mugs and put them in the sink. Then they headed up to their rooms.

Jessie tucked Benny in for the second time that night. "See you in the morning," she said.

"Good night," said Benny. This time he had no trouble falling asleep.

The next morning when Benny awoke, he jumped to his window and looked outside. The rain had stopped and sunlight was sparkling on the wet grass.

He looked over at the boxcar. As far as Benny could tell, it was just as they had left it. He pulled on some clothes and hurried downstairs to the kitchen, where Mrs. McGregor was getting breakfast ready. Henry, Jessie, and Violet were already there, telling Mrs. McGregor what had happened the night before.

"Are you sure you didn't just leave the door to the boxcar open?" Mrs. McGregor asked as she flipped their pancakes. "It could have been a raccoon or a stray dog that went in and knocked things over."

"I'm sure I shut it," said Violet.

"I've encountered some pretty smart raccoons," said Mrs. McGregor, turning to face the children. "Since they can open garbage cans, they can probably open that boxcar door."

"But what about the light I saw?" Benny asked.

"It could have just been a reflection of something," their housekeeper said.

"I guess. . . . " Benny said.

"Was anything broken or missing?" asked Mrs. McGregor.

"No," said Jessie.

"Then I wouldn't worry about it." Mrs. McGregor turned back to the griddle, humming softly.

"I want to take a look at the boxcar in the daylight," Jessie said. "Maybe we'll find some clues."

"I'll come, too," said Benny. They all followed Jessie out the door.

"Hurry back, the pancakes are almost ready," Mrs. McGregor called after them.

Violet couldn't believe how scared she'd felt walking across the yard the night before. In the daylight, it wasn't frightening at all.

Inside the boxcar, the Aldens looked around carefully. They saw no footprints or pawprints or any other clues to help them figure out who had been in the boxcar the night before.

Benny, Violet, Jessie, and Henry knelt to clean up the game pieces that had spilled, then put the boxes back into a neat pile.

There were still a lot of unanswered questions. But at least now the boxcar was back in order.

When the children returned to the sunny kitchen, the pancakes were waiting.

"Everything okay out there?" Mrs. McGregor asked.

"All straightened up," said Jessie.

"That's good," said Mrs. McGregor. "Could you kids walk into town and pick up some groceries after breakfast?"

"Sure," said Violet.

"The list's on the table," Mrs. McGregor said.

A short while later the Aldens were on their way to town, pulling a small red wagon for the groceries.

"I just can't believe that someone sneaked into our boxcar last night," said Violet.

"Maybe Mrs. McGregor was right," said Jessie. "Maybe it was just a raccoon."

Henry shook his head. "Maybe," he said, "but something tells me it was a person."

"But what was a person doing in our box-car in the middle of the night?" asked Benny.

"I don't know," said Henry. "I don't know why anyone would be there. But someone was."

"Professor Murray and Amelia and Claire all seemed really interested in the boxcar," Violet pointed out. "Maybe one of them came back to look at it again."

"In the middle of the night?" Benny said. "Why not just wait until daytime?"

"It does seem pretty unlikely," Violet admitted.

"Unless . . ." Jessie began. "Unless one of them wanted to go in without us knowing about it."

"Why wouldn't they want us to know?" said Benny.

Jessie shrugged. "Beats me."

"Whoever was in there knocked all that stuff over and just left it that way," Henry pointed out. "Wouldn't one of them have picked it up?"

"You're right," said Violet.

They continued walking without saying anything. They were all deep in their own thoughts.

Then Jessie spoke up. "Benny, tell us again what you saw out your window."

"I saw a light," Benny said. "Near the boxcar. It was sort of . . . floating along."

"Floating?" Jessie repeated.

"I'm telling you, it looked ghostly," said Benny.

"Maybe that's it," said Henry.

"You think it was a ghost?" Benny asked, his eyes widening.

"No, but maybe it was someone trying to make us *think* there was a ghost," said Henry. "Maybe someone went in the boxcar and knocked things over to make us think the boxcar was haunted."

"Who would do that?" asked Violet.

"Well, it was Professor Murray who made Benny think the boxcar might be haunted in the first place," Henry said. "Maybe he

did it on purpose. Then he came over with a flashlight in the middle of the night and knocked things over."

"But why would he want us to think the boxcar is haunted?" said Violet.

"Remember how upset he was that we use the boxcar as a playhouse?" said Henry. "Maybe he thinks that if he scares us, we'll want to get rid of it and give it to a museum like he suggested."

"Maybe," said Violet. She didn't sound convinced.

"Well, if he thinks we're going to be scared that easily, he's wrong," said Benny, standing up tall and thrusting out his chest.

"I just don't believe Professor Murray would do something like that," said Jessie. "He is a professor, after all, and he's Ms. Murray's brother. She's so nice—I can't believe her brother would be so sneaky."

"Maybe he thought there was no other way to convince us," said Henry.

"Maybe," said Jessie. "But I wonder more about Amelia."

"What about her?" asked Henry.

"Professor Murray is our neighbor's brother," said Jessie, "but we don't know anything about Amelia — who she is, why she's interested in our boxcar. We don't even know her last name!"

"You're right," Benny said.

"She said she likes old train cars," said Henry. "That doesn't mean she'd break into one."

"But it doesn't mean she wouldn't, either," Jessie said.

"Well, we'll just have to keep our eyes open," Violet said. "Right now we don't have much to go on."

They had reached the door to the grocery store and were about to enter when Benny stopped abruptly. "I have an idea!" he cried. "Let's sleep outside in the boxcar tonight! That way, we'll see if anything unusual happens."

"Great idea," said Henry.

"And if there's a ghost," Benny added, "we'll know for sure."

CHAPTER 5

# Strange Noises

The Aldens went through the grocery store buying everything on Mrs. McGregor's list. Then they returned home, pulling the wagon filled with grocery bags.

"I'll check the mail," called Benny, running to the mailbox. The mail hadn't arrived yet, but there was something in the box. Benny pulled it out. It was a brochure with a note clipped to the front. Benny tried to figure out what the note said, but he was just learning to read, and the note was written in cursive. He would have to ask for help. Benny ran into the house.

When he entered the kitchen, he knew immediately that Mrs. McGregor had been baking. The kitchen smelled delicious. Lines of cookies were cooling on a rack. They were filled with jelly and covered in powdered sugar.

"Those look good," said Benny. "May I have one?"

"Not yet—you'll spoil your lunch," Mrs. McGregor said. She was preparing a big fruit salad.

Disappointed, Benny quickly put his hand down.

"Was there any mail?" Henry asked.

"Just this," said Benny, handing him the brochure.

Henry quickly read the note clipped on top. "It's from Professor Murray. He wrote, '*This might be a good place for your boxcar.*'" Henry removed the note and looked at the brochure. "It's a brochure for a museum near here."

The others moved closer to look at the brochure. "It looks nice, but . . . " said Jessie.

"We're not giving away our boxcar," said Benny. "Grandfather said so. Professor Murray can't make us."

"No, he can't," said Jessie, putting an arm around her brother. "We'll show the brochure to Grandfather when he gets home, but I'm sure he'll agree with us."

"Professor Murray doesn't give up," said Henry.

The others nodded.

Jessie turned to Mrs. McGregor. "Is it all right if we sleep out in the boxcar tonight?"

"That sounds fun," said the housekeeper. "And the weather is supposed to be lovely tonight."

"Great!" said Benny.

After lunch, the children hurried upstairs to pack for their sleepover. They gathered pajamas and slippers and bathrobes and stuffed them into their overnight bags. Then they grabbed sleeping bags and pillows and stuffed animals to sleep with and books to read. At last they came downstairs, their arms filled.

"Oh my goodness!" said Mrs. McGregor

when she saw them. "Are you sure you're only going for one night? Looks like you've got enough to last you through next month!"

The children laughed.

"Mrs. McGregor, about those cookies . . ." Benny said.

"Yes?" said Mrs. McGregor.

"I was just thinking it wouldn't be a real sleepover without a bedtime snack," Benny said.

"I was expecting that," said Mrs. McGregor, handing him a tin. "I've put eight cookies in here—two for each of you. Are you sure you can carry it with all that stuff?"

"Yeah, I'll just tuck my sleeping bag under this arm and my pillow under this arm. . . . " Benny let out a moan as everything fell to the floor.

"Why don't you come back for the cookies?" Mrs. McGregor suggested, hiding a smile. "It's a long way until bedtime."

"Well. . . . Okay," said Benny reluctantly. He followed his brother and sisters out to the boxcar.

"Let's put our stuff in that corner," Jessie said, pointing. "We'll get everything set up tonight when we're ready for bed." The others agreed.

"Now, how about a rematch of that soccer game," suggested Henry.

"You're on," said Violet.

Benny piled his things in the corner with the rest of the sleeping bags and pillows. "I'll be right there," he called to the others, heading back to the house. "I'm going to get the cookies."

Henry, Jessie, and Violet were kicking the ball around when Benny ran back to the boxcar with the cookies. He opened the tin and peeked in. The cookies smelled wonderful. "Maybe I'll just have *one* now," Benny said to himself. He quickly counted to check how many there were. "Eight cookies, just like Mrs. McGregor said." That was good. That meant he could eat one now and still have another one that night. He picked up one of the cookies and took a bite. Delicious.

"Benny, are you coming?" Violet called from the yard.

Benny quickly stuffed the rest of the cookie into his mouth, brushing the powdered sugar from his hands. As he came out of the boxcar, his brother and sisters started laughing.

"What?" Benny asked.

"You didn't by any chance *try* one of the cookies, did you?" Jessie asked, her eyebrows raised.

"Er . . . maybe. . . . " Benny said. "Why?"

"Your mustache gives you away," Jessie said, giggling. Benny smiled and wiped the white powder off his face.

The Aldens played soccer until Mrs. McGregor called them in for lemonade. Afterward, Henry and Jessie went to the family room for a game of checkers.

"I'm going to sit on the porch and read my book," Violet said. She had started a ghost story the day before and was eager to get back to it.

"I'll go get my book, too," Benny said.

"Great," said Violet. "I'll read you some."

Benny ran to the boxcar, where he'd left his book, thinking someone might read him another chapter at bedtime. When he stepped inside, he looked longingly at the tin of cookies on the table.

"No," he told himself. "I already had one. I'll have another one tonight." But then Benny noticed something strange — white powder and crumbs on the table around the tin. "I didn't make *that* much of a mess, did I?" he wondered aloud. Stepping closer, Benny noticed that the lid of the tin wasn't tightly shut. Benny lifted the lid and looked inside.

"Huh!" he said. There were only six cookies in the tin. Mrs. McGregor had put in eight, and he'd eaten one. That meant there should be seven cookies left.

"Hey, they made fun of me for eating a cookie, and now one of them had one!" Benny said. He ran back to the house. "Jessie, Henry?" he called, heading into the family room. "Did you have a cookie?"

"No," said Jessie.

"I'm too stuffed from lunch," said Henry.

Benny went out to the porch. "Violet, did you have a cookie?"

Violet shook her head.

"Are you sure?" Benny asked.

Violet smiled. "Don't you think I'd remember if I'd eaten one?"

"Yes," Benny said. "But . . ." He frowned. "Will you come take a look at something?"

Benny led Violet back to the boxcar and showed her the tin. "Mrs. McGregor told me we could each have two cookies. That would make eight, right?"

"Yes," said Violet.

"I ate one before," said Benny. "Which means there should be seven left. But there are only six cookies now."

Violet looked inside the tin and quickly counted. "You're right."

"If you and Jessie and Henry didn't have any," Benny said, "who ate the missing cookie?"

Violet narrowed her eyes and smiled at her little brother. "Are you sure you didn't have another?"

"No!" Benny said. "They've just been sitting here in the boxcar."

"Maybe Watch took one," said Violet.

"Or some other animal, like Mrs. McGregor said this morning."

"Would an animal take out one cookie and leave the tin here, with the lid on?" asked Benny.

"That does seem unlikely," said Violet.

Benny bit his lip. "You don't think it was the ghost, do you?"

"Oh, Benny, not the ghost again. No, I'm sure there's a logical explanation," said Violet.

Just then Watch appeared in the doorway of the boxcar with his wet, shredded tennis ball in his mouth.

"Hey, boy, you want to play?" Benny asked, plucking the ball from Watch's mouth. He threw the ball out into the yard, and Watch chased after it. Laughing, Benny followed him.

Violet looked at the cookies and shrugged her shoulders. Then she curled up on a chair and opened her book to read.

She hadn't been sitting there long when she heard a strange scuffling sound.

Violet looked around, but seeing nothing unusual, she went back to her book.

A moment later the sound came again. Violet looked up quickly, scanning the boxcar. It sounded like the noise had come from inside, but Violet couldn't figure out what would have made the sound. She was alone with just the table, chairs, stack of games, and all the usual things. And in the corner, the pile of bedding for that night. Was she imagining things?

Violet began reading again, but she found it hard to concentrate. She felt a prickly feeling at the back of her neck, as if someone was watching her.

Suddenly, Violet jerked around, almost certain there was someone behind her.

But the boxcar was empty.

This is silly, Violet thought. Benny's talk of ghosts and this creepy book have got me spooked.

Just then Watch appeared in the doorway, panting and wagging his tail.

Relief flooded over Violet. "Hey, boy!" she said. Watch ran over and she rubbed his head and back. "Are you done playing ball with Benny?"

Then Violet had a thought. "Was that you before, scratching around the outside of the boxcar?" Of course Watch couldn't answer her. He just looked up at her and wagged his tail as she scratched his ears. "That must be what I heard," Violet told herself. But she wasn't completely convinced. Nervously, she took one more look around the boxcar before walking out with Watch.

Stepping out into the bright sunshine, Violet felt silly for having been scared. She raced Watch to the house and got him a dog biscuit from the kitchen.

Leaving him to munch it happily, Violet went to find the others. Jessie and Henry had just finished their checkers game and Benny was about to play the winner.

"I beat Henry," Jessie said.

"But you won't beat me," said Benny, grinning.

"How's the book?" Henry asked.

"It's okay," said Violet. "Um, Benny,

when did you come in from playing with Watch?"

"A little while ago," Benny said as he set up his pieces.

"Did you see him scratching around the boxcar at all?" Violet asked.

"No," said Benny. "Why?"

"Oh, I don't know . . ." Violet said. She felt silly mentioning how spooked she'd felt.

"What's up?" Henry asked.

"Well, it's just that when I was alone in the boxcar, reading, I heard some weird noises," said Violet. "I thought it might have been Watch."

The other three looked back at the board.

"But I had the strangest feeling . . . " Violet went on.

"What kind of feeling?" Henry asked.

"Well, like someone was watching me," said Violet.

"Really? *Inside* the boxcar?" said Benny. "And remember there was that missing cookie!" He quickly told Henry and Jessie about the cookie.

"Let's go out and look around," said Jessie. "Maybe some sort of animal was in there or right outside. Maybe it left some pawprints or scratches."

Leaving their checkers game, the Aldens went back outside. The boxcar looked the way it always did. Benny showed Henry and Jessie the cookie tin. Violet showed them where she'd been sitting when she heard the noises.

"Let's do a thorough search," Jessie suggested.

"Okay," said the others. Following Jessie's lead, they got down on their hands and knees and searched the floor and walls for any animal scratches or muddy pawprints. They looked under the table, behind the chairs, near the stack of games, and under the big pile of sleeping bags, clothes, and stuffed animals in the corner. There was nothing.

Jessie stopped searching and looked around at the others. "We thought Amelia or Professor Murray could have been poking around in the boxcar last night," she said. "But I don't think either of them would steal a cookie, do you?"

"That doesn't seem likely," Henry agreed. He stared at the wall, deep in thought. Suddenly he noticed something.

Henry looked from one corner of the boxcar to the corner opposite. "That's weird," he said.

"What's weird?" asked Jessie.

Henry looked back and forth again. "I can't believe we never noticed this before."

"Noticed *what*?" asked Benny, bursting with curiosity.

"See how, down in this corner, there's a diagonal wall?" Henry pointed to the corner where the pile of sleeping bags was. "But that corner doesn't have it." Henry pointed to the opposite corner. "It's almost as if extra boards were added in this corner." Henry tapped the wall and raised his eyebrows. "It's hollow!"

"I don't get it," said Benny.

"There's a space between these boards and the wall. A hollow space," Henry explained.

"You think someone just added a secret compartment to the boxcar?" Jessie said.

"No," Henry said. "If the boards had just been added, they would look fresh and new. But these boards are faded to the same color as the rest of the boxcar walls. That means they must have been nailed into place a long time ago."

"Why?" asked Violet.

"I'm not sure," said Henry. "Maybe this space was once used to store something."

"But there's no handle or doorknob," Jessie pointed out. "No way to get in there easily."

"That's just what I was thinking," said Henry, staring at the corner.

"Why would someone want a compartment that you can't get into?" asked Benny.

"Good question," said Jessie. She looked puzzled.

Henry spoke up. "It would be the perfect place . . . to *hide* something."

CHAPTER 6

# A Treasure Hunt

The children stared at the corner of the boxcar.

"A place to hide something?" Jessie repeated. "To hide what?"

"That's what I want to find out," Henry said. He peered closely at the nails holding the boards in place. Then he ran out of the boxcar.

"Where — " Jessie called after him. But he was already gone.

Henry ran straight to Grandfather's workshop. He grabbed a hammer and returned to the boxcar.

"What's that for?" Violet asked when she saw what Henry was holding.

"I'm going to pry out the nails holding the boards. Then we can see what's behind there," Henry said excitedly.

"Wait a minute," said Jessie. "Remember Professor Murray said our boxcar is a valuable antique. First we should ask Mrs. McGregor if it's okay."

Henry sighed. He was eager to see what was hidden in that compartment and didn't want to wait. But he knew Jessie was right. "All right."

Jessie ran into the house. The others waited impatiently for her return. At last she came running back across the grass.

"She said it's okay, as long as we're very careful," Jessie said. "She said it could always be nailed back into place."

"Great!" said Henry. One by one, Henry pried off all the nails holding the board in place. He took off the board and looked down into the narrow space behind.

"What do you see?" Benny asked eagerly.

"It's too dark," Henry said after a moment. "I can't see anything." He began removing the nails from the next board. As he pulled out the last nail, the board began to tilt forward. Henry caught the board and set it on the floor.

The children were quite surprised to see what was hidden inside.

On the floor in the corner sat an old-fashioned rag doll. She was made completely of cloth, with thick brown yarn for hair. Her face had been stitched on with colored threads. She wore a faded dress with an apron on top. Henry carefully picked up the doll. After looking at it for a moment, he handed it to Jessie, who held it delicately and examined its hair and face.

"A *doll*?" said Benny. "Why would a doll be in a secret compartment?"

"I wonder who this belonged to," Jessie said in a hushed voice. She handed the doll to Violet, who cradled it gently in her arms.

"How long do you think she's been hidden there?" asked Violet. "She looks very old."

"And worn out," added Benny.

"It looks like someone loved this doll very much," said Violet.

"It must have been hidden here a long time ago," said Henry. "See how much darker the walls of the boxcar are behind where I removed the boards? That's because the sunlight faded the rest of the walls. Seems to me this compartment must have been closed up for a long time."

"I wonder if the person who came here last night was looking for this doll," said Jessie.

"How would anybody know about her?" Violet asked.

"I don't know," Jessie said. "But Professor Murray and Amelia both seemed so interested in looking at our boxcar. I'm wondering if maybe the boxcar wasn't the only thing that interested them."

"Do you think the doll is valuable?" asked Violet.

"That old thing?" said Benny, looking surprised.

"Some old things are worth a lot of money," Jessie explained.

Henry had another idea. "Maybe whoever broke into the boxcar has some connection to the doll."

Benny's eyes widened. "You think whoever hid it here came back to get it? And stole a cookie?"

Henry smiled and shook his head. "No, whoever hid the doll here must have done it long ago, before we even found the boxcar. And I don't think it's related to the cookie."

Violet stroked the doll's soft hair and fluffed her little dress. As she was smoothing the doll's apron she felt something inside the tiny pocket. "What's this?" she asked, pulling out a scrap of paper. Violet set the doll in her lap and carefully unfolded the paper. "It says, *Dig next to the doorstep.*" She held the note out for the others to see.

"*Dig next to the doorstep?*" repeated Henry. "But what — "

"It's a treasure hunt!" Benny said excitedly. "We're supposed to dig next to the doorstep to find the treasure!" He quickly got to his feet. "Let's go!"

Benny jumped out the door and followed the others. They stood looking at the stump they used as a doorstep.

But suddenly Henry said, "Wait a minute. If this doll was hidden a long time ago, then this is the wrong doorstep."

"What do you mean?" asked Violet.

"Remember, the boxcar didn't used to be here," Henry reminded them. "Grandfather moved it for us."

"You're right!" said Jessie. "If we want to dig next to the doorstep, we have to go back to Silver City where the boxcar used to be!"

"Can we?" Benny asked.

"Sure," said Jessie. "Silver City isn't too far from here. We could get there on our bicycles." She looked at her watch. "But I think it will have to wait until tomorrow. It's nearly dinnertime."

"All right," said Henry. "Sounds like tomorrow will be an adventure."

The children all smiled at one another. Violet looked down at the doll that she was still holding and gave it a gentle hug.

When they went inside for dinner, the Aldens showed Mrs. McGregor the doll.

"She looks like a very old doll," said the housekeeper.

When they told her about the note in the doll's apron pocket, Mrs. McGregor's eyes widened. "Sounds like a treasure hunt," she said.

"That's what I thought!" said Benny.

"Tomorrow we'd like to go back to the place where the boxcar was before," Jessie said.

"Sounds exciting," said Mrs. McGregor. "I can't wait to hear what you find!"

After they'd eaten, the children went out to the boxcar. They were excited to camp out. They waved to Professor Murray and Claire, who were just getting out of a car and going into the house next door.

"Did you get the brochure I left you?" Professor Murray called.

"Yes," said Jessie. "Thank you."

"What do you think?" he asked.

The children looked at one another.

"It was . . . interesting," said Henry. "We'll show it to our grandfather."

"Good," said Professor Murray. "It's a wonderful museum. I think it would be just the right place for your boxcar."

The Murrays went into the house.

"He just keeps on trying," said Henry as they went into the boxcar. "Convincing us to give up the boxcar seems really important to him."

The Aldens put on their pajamas. They arranged their sleeping bags and pillows in two neat lines. Henry's and Benny's sleeping bags were blue, Jessie's was red, and of course Violet's was purple, with tiny purple flowers on the soft flannel lining. Jessie placed their flashlight in the center of the sleeping bags, and its cozy light filled the boxcar.

"Now can we have the cookies?" Benny asked. He had gotten an extra one from Mrs. McGregor to replace the missing one.

"Not yet," said Violet. "I'll be right back." She ran back to the house.

"What is she doing?" Benny asked. "I've been waiting all day for my other cookie."

Henry and Jessie shrugged.

When Violet returned, she was holding a pitcher of cold milk and a stack of paper cups.

"Good thinking!" Jessie said. Picking up the flashlight, she walked over to the corner where they'd left the cookie tin.

As she walked back with the tin, Benny said, "Wait a minute!"

"I thought you wanted a cookie right away," Jessie said.

"I do, but I just realized something," Benny explained. "See how the flashlight beam seems to kind of float as Jessie carries it? The light I saw last night moved like that, too."

"Maybe that's what it was," said Henry. "Maybe someone was over here carrying a flashlight."

"That explains why the light was bouncing along like that," Benny said.

"But we still don't know who it was," Violet reminded him.

Jessie set the cookie tin next to the flashlight in the center of all the sleeping bags. Violet poured each of them a cup of milk. They all sat on their sleeping bags and enjoyed the bedtime treat. Watch lay curled up on his flannel blanket in the corner.

"I can't wait until tomorrow when we go back to where the boxcar used to be," said Benny, licking crumbs from his fingers.

"I wonder what we'll find there," said Violet. She stroked the rag doll, which she had placed beside her pillow.

"Remember how happy we were to find the boxcar?" Jessie said. "It was about to rain, and we needed shelter."

"You and Jessie looked inside first to make sure it was okay," said Violet. "Then we all ran inside, and it made such a warm, dry little house."

"I remember that," said Benny, grinning. He gulped down the last of his milk.

"I wonder what we'll find when we dig," said Henry.

"I can't wait to see!" Benny said.

When they'd finished eating, they all went back in the house and washed their hands and faces and brushed their teeth. Then they said good night to Mrs. McGregor.

"Sleep well," she called after them. "Wake me if you need anything."

Once they were in the boxcar, Jessie slid the door almost all the way closed. She left it open a crack to let in fresh air.

"I wonder if anything unusual will happen here tonight," said Benny. He climbed into his sleeping bag and snuggled down deep.

"We'll soon find out," said Henry. He picked up Benny's book and read him the next chapter. "Now try to sleep."

"I'm too excited," said Benny.

"Just try," Henry said, rolling over with his own book.

Benny's thoughts were racing. What would they find when they dug near the old doorstep? Would anything strange happen that night? But he was so tired he soon fell asleep.

* * *

When the Aldens woke, a thin line of sunlight was streaming through the door crack.

"It's morning," Benny said with a yawn. "And no ghosts came last night."

"You sound disappointed," said Jessie, stretching.

"I guess I am," Benny replied.

The children hurried to dress and roll up their sleeping bags.

"Good morning," said Mrs. McGregor when they came in for breakfast. "How was your night?"

"It was fine," said Henry.

"No ghosts," said Benny.

Mrs. McGregor smiled.

The children ate quickly because they were eager to be on their way.

"Let's bring a lunch with us," Jessie suggested. "We can have a picnic there."

"Good idea," the others agreed. Jessie and Benny got out bread and ham and made sandwiches. Henry filled a thermos with lemonade and found some cups. Violet added fresh peaches. They put all the food into Jessie's backpack and grabbed the picnic blanket.

When they said good-bye to Mrs. McGregor, she handed them something wrapped in foil.

"What's this?" asked Jessie.

"You can't let the rest of those good cookies go to waste," said the housekeeper.

"No, we certainly can't," Jessie agreed, tucking the cookies into her backpack with the rest of their lunch.

Henry grabbed a shovel from the garden shed, and they set off on their bicycles.

They were just heading out of the driveway when they saw Claire and her father walking across their yard.

"Hi!" called Violet.

Claire smiled shyly. "Hi."

"We're riding over to Silver City," said Violet. "Want to join us?"

Claire's smile faded. "I don't have a bike here."

"That's too bad," said Violet.

"I was just going over to say hello to your grandfather," Professor Murray said.

"He's away on business," said Henry.

"Still?" said the professor. "You must miss him when he's gone."

The Aldens nodded. "But we like it when he comes back!" Benny said.

"Claire doesn't like it when I travel either," said Professor Murray. "She has bad dreams about ghosts."

Claire blushed. "Just sometimes," she said softly.

Professor Murray smiled. "Do you kids ever worry about ghosts?"

"Not really," said Benny.

"Claire, we'll come by when we get back, and maybe you can play then," Violet suggested.

"Okay," said Claire, her smile returning. The Aldens waved good-bye and pedaled off. When they were out of hearing distance, Jessie turned to the others. "Don't you think it's a little strange how Professor Murray keeps talking about ghosts?" she said.

"I noticed that, too," said Henry. "If he is the one 'haunting' the boxcar, he wants us to be scared — scared enough to sell it to a museum."

No one knew what to say to that. So they just kept riding.

The ride to Silver City was long, but it was a beautiful day. The children pedaled along happily, enjoying the sunshine, the blue sky, and the flowers and trees around them.

At last they came to the woods where the boxcar had been. Tall old trees reached up into the sky. Overgrown bushes were everywhere.

"This is the place," said Jessie excitedly, leading the way.

The children walked their bikes into the woods, pushing branches out of the way as they went. After a little while they came to a large open area. Rusty train tracks cut through the middle. Grass and bushes grew over the tracks.

"Here's where the boxcar was," Henry said, leading the way.

"And look, this is where the stump used to be," said Jessie, pointing to the spot.

"Do you remember how Benny was afraid to live in the boxcar at first?" said Henry. "He was worried the engine would come take us away."

They all laughed at that.

"There's the brook where we used to wash," Violet said, pointing. The children ran over and dipped their hands in the cold, clear water.

Suddenly Benny remembered why they were there. "Well, if this is where the stump was," he said, "then this is where we should dig!"

"You're right," said Henry, unfastening the shovel, which he had strapped onto the back of his bike. "Let's get started."

Henry began digging on one side of where the stump had been. The ground was hard, making it a tough job.

After he had dug a fairly large hole, he stopped and looked at the others. So far, they'd found nothing. "Maybe it's the other side," he said.

"I guess so," said Jessie. "I'll do some now." She took the shovel and began digging.

Benny was beginning to worry that maybe there would be no treasure after all.

Jessie was about to give up digging when the shovel hit something hard. She stopped and looked at the others. "Either I've hit a big rock, or we've just found something."

Digging more slowly now, she carefully uncovered a smooth square of metal.

"Look at that!" cried Benny.

Jessie dug around the four sides of the square to reveal a metal box. When she had cleared a lot of the dirt away, Henry bent down and grabbed hold of the box. He pulled, but it was still too deep in the ground. It didn't budge.

Jessie dug a little more dirt out and Henry tried again. This time the box came up.

"At last!" Benny cried. "We've found the treasure!"

CHAPTER 7

## Inside the Box

Henry set the box down gently beside the hole.

"Is it heavy?" asked Benny excitedly.

"No, it's not," said Henry.

"What's inside?" Benny asked.

"We'll soon see." Reaching around in front, Henry carefully unlatched the top. Then he lifted the lid.

Inside the box there was only one object. It was a leatherbound book.

"A book?" said Benny. "What kind of treasure is that?"

Violet grinned. "I think books are the best kind of treasure there is!"

Jessie carefully lifted the book from the box. It looked very old and delicate. She opened the cover and read aloud, "*My Story, by Isabel Wile.*"

"It's handwritten," said Violet, peering over her sister's shoulder. "It looks like a diary."

Jessie turned to the next page. "You're right. Isabel Wile's diary, I guess. I wonder who she was."

"There's a date on the first page," Violet pointed out. "Wow, this was written a long time ago!"

"Isabel must have been the owner of the doll," Henry said. "She wrote the diary, buried it here, and put the note in the doll's apron. Then she hid the doll in the boxcar."

"And we found it!" cried Benny.

"I wonder why she did all that," said Jessie.

"Maybe if we read the diary we'll find out," said Henry.

"Is it okay to read someone else's diary?" Violet asked.

"In this case it is," Jessie assured her. "This diary is very old and it seems that Isabel — or somebody — wanted us to find it."

"Okay," said Benny. "Only . . . could we eat our lunch first?"

"Sure," Henry said. The bike ride and all the digging had made them hungry.

The children washed their hands in the stream, just as they had when they'd lived there. Then they spread out the picnic blanket beside the space where the boxcar had been. Jessie gave everyone a napkin and Violet passed out the sandwiches. Henry poured lemonade for all of them.

"Shall I start reading the diary?" Jessie asked, once she had eaten some of her sandwich.

The others nodded eagerly.

"*June 2*," Jessie began. "*Papa still has not found another job. We can no longer pay the rent on our apartment, so we've had to move out. But the good news is, Mama and Papa* have found us a wonderful place to stay. It's an old boxcar."

"Isabel lived in *our* boxcar?" said Benny, his eyes wide.

"Actually, I think we lived in *her* boxcar," said Henry. "She was there first."

"Go on," Violet urged.

"*It is snug and dry inside,*" Jessie read. "*Mama folded up some blankets and made a cozy bed for me and Rebecca on the floor in one corner. Louis is sleeping in the other corner. Mama and Papa have a bed along the front wall.*"

"Rebecca and Louis must be her sister and brother," Violet said.

Jessie read, "*We had our first dinner in the boxcar tonight. We sat on the ground like a picnic and ate bread and cheese and milk.*"

"Sounds like what we used to eat," said Henry.

Jessie went on, "*And for dessert we picked blueberries.*"

"Hey! I remember those bushes," said Benny, springing to his feet. "There they are — still full of berries."

"Let's pick some!" said Jessie, setting the diary aside.

They collected a large bunch of blueberries in a napkin and ate them with the peaches and the delicious cookies.

"Just as sweet as I remembered them," said Henry, popping a large handful of blueberries into his mouth.

Jessie continued reading. "*Soon Papa will find a new job, and we'll be in a regular house again. But for now, it's fun living here in the woods, in our little boxcar home.*"

"That's what we thought, too," said Benny.

Jessie turned the page and began the next entry. "*Today Rebecca got covered in mud, so Mama told me to give her a bath in the stream. I don't think she liked it very much.*"

"Rebecca must be her *little* sister," said Benny.

"This sounds odd," said Jessie. "It says, '*I put Rebecca on a rock to dry.*'"

"That *is* strange," said Violet.

"*Then Papa took me to the library,*" Jessie

read. *"I got a new mystery story. I'll read it to Rebecca tonight. Then maybe tomorrow Rebecca and I can make up our own mystery."*

"Hey, Isabel likes mysteries, just like us!" said Benny.

Jessie went on to the next entry. *"Today I cut Rebecca's hair. Mama was very angry with me."*

"I'll bet she was," said Henry with a laugh.

*"Mama reminded me that Rebecca's hair won't grow back."* Jessie stopped and looked at the others.

"That's *really* weird," said Benny.

Jessie read ahead a little bit and then she started to laugh. "Now I get it! Listen to this — *'Mama gave me some thick brown yarn to make Rebecca some more hair.'* Rebecca must be her *doll!*"

"That's the doll we found!" said Violet. "That's Rebecca."

Jessie read several more entries from Isabel's diary. Isabel and Rebecca had lots of fun together, making up mysteries to solve.

Sometimes Isabel played with Louis. They helped her mother keep the boxcar clean and cook the meals. Their father was usually off looking for a new job. At night, they would read mysteries together.

The children were all enjoying Isabel's story, but it was getting late. At last Jessie closed the book, marking her place with a leaf. "We'd better head home."

"Yes," said Henry. "Mrs. McGregor will be worried."

"I can't wait to show her the diary," said Violet.

The Aldens packed up what was left of their lunch and put it in Jessie's backpack, along with the diary. Then they rode home.

When the children were just up the street from their house, Violet slowed down.

"Tired?" Jessie asked.

"No, look," her sister said, motioning to the car parked in front of the Aldens' house. It was a little purple car. "Do you think that's Amelia?"

Jessie nodded. "How many people drive purple cars?"

"I wonder what she's doing here," Violet said.

As the Aldens rode up alongside the car, they could see that no one was inside.

"Hey, look!" Benny cried, pointing into Amelia's car. "A flashlight!"

"Maybe she's going camping," said Violet. "I see she has a sleeping bag, too."

"Or maybe she's the one who was snooping around the boxcar at night," Benny said.

"Maybe . . . but lots of people have flashlights," Jessie reminded him.

Just then the Aldens saw Amelia walking across their front lawn. She looked surprised when she saw them near her car, but then she waved.

"Hello!" Amelia called as she got closer. "I hope you don't mind — I was just taking another look at your boxcar."

The Aldens looked at one another. She was back to look at it *again*? And she'd just walked into their backyard without asking?

As if she'd heard what they were thinking, Amelia said, "I asked Mrs. McGregor if it was okay, and she said yes."

"Sure, that's fine," said Jessie.

"Say, have you ever found anything . . . unusual in the boxcar?" Amelia asked.

"Unusual?" Henry repeated. "Like what?"

"Oh, I don't know . . . never mind," said Amelia with a quick smile. "I'd better get going now." She got into her car and drove off.

The Aldens walked their bikes up the driveway.

"Do you think she was trying to ask about the doll?" asked Violet.

The others shrugged their shoulders, uncertain. "How would she know about it?" Jessie said.

They had reached the garage and were putting their bikes away and hanging up their helmets.

"Well, there must be *some* reason she keeps coming back to look at our boxcar," said Benny. "*Especially* if she was there in the middle of the night."

"I don't know what it is," said Jessie, "but I think there's something Amelia is not telling us."

When the Aldens went inside, Mrs. McGregor was setting the table for dinner. "Amelia was just here to look at the boxcar," she told them.

"We saw her as she was coming out," said Violet.

"Look what we found!" said Jessie, taking off her backpack and pulling out the diary.

Mrs. McGregor put down the silverware she was holding and looked at the diary in amazement. "Oh my! You really did find a treasure."

Jessie handed the diary to Mrs. McGregor. She took it and studied the cover carefully before opening it and turning the pages very gently.

"Isabel Wile," Mrs. McGregor said to herself. "I wonder who she was."

"The doll we found belonged to her," Violet said.

"She lived in the boxcar," said Benny. "*Our* boxcar!"

"Isn't that amazing!" Mrs. McGregor said. "Did you read her diary?"

"Part of it," said Jessie. "Until it was time to come home for dinner."

"Which reminds me . . . " Mrs. McGregor said, giving the diary back and hurrying into the kitchen.

After washing their hands, the Aldens finished setting the table as Mrs. McGregor brought in a steaming hot casserole.

"Oh no, I just remembered," said Violet, "we told Claire we'd come by when we got home."

"Now it's too late," said Henry. "We can stop by there tomorrow."

"But let's not tell her about the diary yet," said Jessie.

"Why not?" Benny asked.

"I would rather show it to Grandfather first," Jessie said. "We'll see what he thinks before we tell anyone else."

The others agreed.

That night the children decided to sleep

in the house. Even Benny was now convinced that the strange things in the boxcar probably weren't caused by a ghost. Also, they were tired from their long bike ride to Silver City and wanted the comfort of their own beds.

"Can you read me some of the diary?" Benny asked Jessie as she tucked him into bed.

"In the morning," Jessie said. "I'm too tired now. Besides, we shouldn't read it without the others." She shut Benny's door behind her.

In his room, Henry was just getting into bed when a light in the backyard caught his attention. He went to the window and raised the shade.

"Benny was right!" he said to himself.

CHAPTER 8

# The Light Returns

From his window, Henry could see a light that seemed to float across the yard. He raced down the stairs and opened the back door as quickly as he could, hoping to catch the "ghost" before whoever it was disappeared.

The light stopped bobbing across the yard and suddenly went out. In the darkness, Henry could make out the figure of a person in the middle of the yard. Suddenly the figure began to run, and Henry could hear the sound of pounding footsteps as the person faded into the darkness.

"Hey! Stop!" Henry called out. But whoever it was had disappeared.

A moment later, Jessie appeared on the stairs in her robe. "What happened?" she asked. She joined Henry in the open doorway.

"Someone was sneaking across our yard," Henry said. "I saw a light moving toward the boxcar. But as soon as I opened the door, whoever it was turned the light off and ran away. I guess I surprised him."

"Him?" Jessie repeated. "So you don't think it was Amelia? Remember, she had that flashlight in her car!"

"Maybe," said Henry. "Except for one thing. The person ran off toward the Murrays'."

"Really?" Jessie said, her eyes wide. "So you think it was Claire or Professor Murray?"

"I don't know," said Henry. "It was too dark to see for sure. But it definitely wasn't Claire — the person I saw was an adult."

Henry and Jessie stood looking out at the

dark yard together. After a little while, they stepped back into the house and shut the door.

"I don't think he or she will come back tonight," Henry said.

"We can tell the others in the morning," Jessie said. "No point in waking them now. They had a long day."

"So did we," said Henry. "Let's go back to bed."

The next morning Henry told Benny and Violet what he had seen the night before.

"What would Professor Murray have been doing in our yard in the middle of the night?" asked Violet.

"He was going to the boxcar again," said Benny. "But why does he want to see it in the middle of the night?"

"And why doesn't he just ask our permission?" said Violet.

"Maybe we were right before, maybe he's trying to scare us so we will give away the boxcar," said Henry.

Jessie frowned at her brother. "I can't believe that."

"Should we do something?" Violet asked.

"Let's see if everything is okay in the boxcar," Jessie suggested.

As they ran across the lawn, Watch joined them.

"Come on, boy," Benny said.

The boxcar door was shut. When they rolled it open, everything inside was in its place.

"No harm done," Henry said. "I have a feeling that whoever it was, I scared him or her off last night. They were moving pretty fast."

"Do you think this has anything to do with the diary?" asked Jessie.

"How could it? No one even knows about the diary," Violet pointed out.

"But maybe someone does. . . ." Jessie said.

"Speaking of the diary, can we read the rest of it?" Benny asked. "I want to know what happened to Isabel."

"Yeah, me too," said Henry and Violet.

"I'll go get it," said Jessie.

The other children settled down on the floor of the boxcar. Watch lay down beside Benny.

Jessie came back a few minutes later with the diary. She sat down and opened it. Flipping the pages, she mumbled, "Now where were we? Oh, here."

Jessie read about how Isabel and Rebecca had played together during the hot summer days. One day they found a tiny kitten in the woods. *"She's black with a white line down her nose and a white tummy. Her paws are white. I'm going to call her Mittens. Mama says I can keep her."*

"She found a kitten, and we found a dog!" said Benny, rubbing Watch's belly.

"Remember when we found Watch?" said Jessie, looking up from the diary. "He had a thorn in his foot."

"You removed it," Violet recalled. "And he's been our pet ever since."

Jessie turned the page. "This entry is dated August 15. Hey, it's good news!" She read aloud, *"Papa has found a job! We are so happy. Mama has found us a small apartment and soon school will begin again."*

Jessie read on. The next entry was from the following day. *"We are packing up our things and leaving this cozy boxcar. I'll miss it."*

"We missed it, too," said Benny. "We were so glad when Grandfather moved it here."

Jessie continued reading, *"I'm going to leave this diary here, because this part of my life is ending. Mama says I'm getting too big to play with dolls, so Rebecca is going to stay here, too. Louis will help me make her a special hiding place with some wood we found. I'll bury the diary and put a note in Rebecca's pocket. I hope some day someone else will live in the boxcar and find Rebecca. She will lead them on a mystery."*

"That's just what happened!" said Benny.

Jessie read the last line. *"I hope other children will enjoy the mystery I've left behind."* Jessie closed the diary.

"Is that all there is?" asked Benny.

"Yes," said Jessie.

"But what happened to Isabel's family? Were they okay?" Benny wanted to know.

"I think so," Jessie said. "Her father found a new job and the family left the boxcar for a new home — just like we did."

The children all thought about Isabel and her family.

"I wish we could find out what happened next," Benny said, frowning.

"Well," Henry said thoughtfully. "Maybe there is a way."

"How?" the others asked.

"We could go ask Professor Murray," he said.

"Professor Murray?" Jessie repeated. "You really do think he knows about the diary!"

"No, it's not that," said Henry. "He's a historian. His job is studying the past. Remember he said he's in Greenfield to do research. Maybe we could go to the library and do our own research—about Isabel."

"But she wasn't famous," said Jessie. "They wouldn't have a book about her."

"No, but maybe Professor Murray might have some ideas about where else to look for information," Henry said.

"Yes, he might," Jessie said. "Good idea, Henry."

"And maybe while we're there, we could ask Claire to play with us," Violet suggested.

The Aldens told Mrs. McGregor where they were going, and a few minutes later they were ringing the bell at the Murrays' house.

Florence Murray opened the door. "Hello!" she said, a big smile on her face. "I'll go get Claire."

She started up the stairs, calling for Claire.

Jessie said, "And is Professor Murray home, too?"

Ms. Murray turned around. "Yes, why do you ask?"

"We have a question for him," Henry said.

"He's on the phone, but I'll tell him you're here," Ms. Murray said. "Why don't you sit down in the living room?"

"Thanks," said Henry.

Henry, Jessie, and Benny went into the living room while Violet waited for Claire at the foot of the stairs. After a few minutes, Claire came down the stairs slowly, a shy smile on her face.

"Hi!" said Violet.

"Hello," Claire replied.

"Want to play some soccer?" Violet asked.

"Sure," Claire said.

Violet told the others she and Claire would be outside.

As they walked toward the Aldens', Violet said, "We're going to the library later if you want to come."

"Thanks," said Claire, "but I was there yesterday with my dad. My aunt took out a bunch of books for me."

They went into the garage to get a ball.

"I love to read," Violet said.

Claire smiled. "I know."

Violet was surprised by her comment.

Claire stammered, "I mean, I do, too." Then she paused. "I bet your boxcar is a great place to read."

"Yes, it is," said Violet. She frowned

slightly, still wondering what Claire had meant when she said, "I know."

But before Violet could say anything else, Claire had picked out a soccer ball and was dribbling it into the backyard.

"Come on!" she called to Violet.

Meanwhile, at Florence Murray's house, Professor Murray had just finished his phone call.

He came down the stairs and into the living room. "Hello," he said to the Aldens. "Florence said you wanted to see me?"

Henry said, "We've come to ask your advice."

"About giving that boxcar to the museum?" he asked, looking pleased.

"No, actually, it's not that," Henry said. Professor Murray frowned.

"We want to learn about someone who lived a long time ago," Henry explained, "but we're not sure where to look."

"Who?" the professor asked.

"Nobody famous," Henry said quickly. "Just a local woman. How would we get information about her?"

"Try the local library," Professor Murray said. "Ask the librarian to look her up, see if there are any records of her or her family. If that doesn't work, you can always look at old newspapers and see what you find."

"Old newspapers!" said Jessie. "That's a great idea."

"Thanks, Professor Murray!" said Henry. He led the others outside.

They found Violet and Claire playing soccer in the Aldens' backyard. They joined in and played a lively game until lunchtime.

"I guess I'd better head back to my aunt's," Claire said.

"See you later!" the Aldens called.

After a bite to eat, they told Mrs. McGregor they were going to the library to see what they could learn about Isabel Wile.

"I can't wait to see what you find," Mrs. McGregor said.

"Neither can we," Benny said with a grin. "It's like another treasure hunt!"

CHAPTER 9

# Going Back in Time

When the Aldens arrived at the library, they put their bikes in the bike rack and went inside. They walked straight up to the librarian's desk.

A woman with brown hair approached them. "Hello," she said with a big smile. "I'm Mrs. Shumate. May I help you?"

"We're looking for information about someone who lived in this area a long time ago," Henry said. "Her name was Isabel Wile."

"She may have lived in Silver City," said Jessie.

The librarian pulled out a large book and flipped through it. "What years did she live here?"

Jessie told her the date that was in the diary. "That's when she was a child."

"I don't see anything in the town record," said Mrs. Shumate.

The Aldens were very disappointed.

"Now we'll never know what happened to her," said Benny.

"Wait a minute," said Jessie. "Professor Murray mentioned old newspapers also."

"Oh, yes," said Mrs. Shumate. "We have the last fifty years of the *Greenfield-Silver City Gazette* on microfilm."

"Microfilm?" Benny repeated. "What's that?"

"I'll show you," said the librarian.

The children followed Mrs. Shumate to a strange-looking machine. It had a large glass screen and some knobs down below.

"If we kept newspapers from a long time ago, the paper would turn yellow and start to crumble," Mrs. Shumate explained. "So we take a picture of every page. Those pictures are side by side on rolls of film. To look at them, you put the roll on this viewer." The librarian snapped a roll into place and flipped a switch on the machine. The front page of the Greenfield-Silver City Gazette appeared on the screen.

"Wow!" said Benny. "Neat."

"Look how old that newspaper is," said Jessie. "There's a horse and carriage in that picture."

"This is the year you asked for," said Mrs. Shumate.

"So that's what the town was like when Isabel was a little girl," Violet said, her eyes widening as she looked at the screen.

"I feel like we've gone back in time!" said Benny.

"To get to the next page, you turn this knob and the roll of film moves forward," the librarian explained.

"We're interested in what happened that spring and summer," said Jessie.

"I'll just push this knob," Mrs. Shumate said. The pictures on the screen whizzed by in a blur. When she stopped pushing the knob, a page came into focus. "March," she said.

"Great," said Jessie. "We'll start looking there."

"If you want to make a copy of a page, just press this button," Mrs. Shumate explained. "It will print out over here."

"Thanks," said Jessie.

"Let me know if you need anything," Mrs. Shumate said with a smile and walked off to help someone else.

"What exactly are we looking for?" asked Violet.

"The diary starts in June. Mr. Wile must have lost his job a few months before, since they'd run out of money," Jessie said. "Maybe we can find out what was happening in town then and why Mr. Wile lost his job."

"Good thinking," said Henry.

The children looked at the front page of the first newspaper in March.

"The mayor was sick," said Violet, reading a headline.

"The garden club had a meeting," Henry said.

Jessie turned the knob, and the pages flicked past. There were lots of interesting articles, ads, and pictures. "I don't see anything that gives us clues about the Wile family." She sounded frustrated. "I hope these newspapers are going to tell us *something*."

"I think they're pretty neat," said Violet. "Look at that ad for shoes! Those don't look anything like what we wear today."

"But I want to learn something about the Wiles." Jessie frowned and turned to the next week's paper.

That newspaper had a huge headline on the front page. "I think we may have found a clue," said Henry.

The headline read, FIRE AT GREENFIELD FACTORY.

"You think the fire has something to do with the Wiles?" Violet asked.

"Look at the smaller headline below." Henry pointed.

HUNDREDS OF PEOPLE OUT OF WORK, it said.

"So maybe that's why Isabel's dad lost his job!" said Violet. "He might have worked at that factory. When the building burned down, he lost his job, along with many other people."

"How sad," said Jessie. "That's why they had to move out of their house and live in the boxcar."

"But he found a new job," said Benny. "Remember the end of the diary?"

"Yes, he did," Jessie said. "Let's print this page, and then we'll keep looking."

The Aldens scanned through the next few weeks of newspapers. They didn't find anything that helped explain what had happened to the Wiles. But they did find out what Greenfield and Silver City had been like a long time ago.

They had come to the middle of August when there was another large headline: NEW FACTORY OPENS IN SILVER CITY.

"I wonder if that's where Mr. Wile found a job," Jessie said. She read the article aloud. It was about a new clothing factory that opened and provided lots of jobs. Jessie printed a copy of that page, too.

The Aldens looked through a few more newspapers until they had reached September. They were growing tired of looking at the old papers on the screen.

"I guess we'll never know for sure what happened to the Wiles," said Henry. "But it looks like Isabel's dad might have gotten a job in the new factory, and that's good."

They rewound the microfilm and returned it to the librarian's desk. Jessie folded the pages they'd copied and tucked them carefully into her backpack.

As they rode home on their bicycles, Jessie said, "I wish we could know for sure what happened to Isabel."

"Me too," said Violet. "But at least now we know that Professor Murray was right— the boxcar *is* haunted."

"What?" said the others, surprised.

"Oh, not by ghosts," Violet said quickly. "It's haunted by the happy memory of the Wile family, who made it their home."

* * *

Later that afternoon, Violet went to put Rebecca in the boxcar. "It's where she belongs," Violet told the others.

Entering the boxcar, Violet saw immediately that someone else had been there. "Not again!" she said.

Violet ran back to tell the others, who came out to see at once.

"Looks like just this one chair was knocked over," said Jessie, picking it up. She also picked up a book that was lying on the floor. It had a plastic cover and the words GREENFIELD LIBRARY stamped on the front.

"Whose is this?" she asked, holding up the book.

"Not mine," said Benny.

Henry and Violet shook their heads, too.

"None of you took this out of the library?" Jessie asked.

"No," they all said.

"Then it must belong to the person who was in here," said Jessie.

"I think you're right," Henry agreed.

"I have a feeling it was Claire," Violet said, taking the book from her sister and turning the pages.

"Really?" asked Jessie. "How do you know?"

"It's a kids' book — a chapter book. Claire and I were just talking about books today. She said she'd gotten a bunch of books at the library, and that she thought the boxcar would be a great place to read," Violet said. "She must have come in while we were gone."

"If she was here today, she might have come here other times without us knowing," said Henry. "Maybe she's the one who's been 'haunting' it."

"But why?" asked Benny.

"I bet she comes because she wants to play," Violet said. "She's probably bored hanging out with her father and her aunt all day."

"But why not just ask if we want to play with her?" Benny said.

"Because she's very shy," Violet said. "I know what that feels like. I think she comes over, hoping to join us, and then maybe gets scared."

"So *she* took the cookie," said Benny.

"No one can resist Mrs. McGregor's cookies," Jessie reminded him. "You know that better than anyone."

"That's true," said Benny, smiling.

"And that day I heard the noises in the boxcar, that could have been Claire," said Violet. "Remember how we had a big pile of sleeping bags in here that day? She must have gotten scared when she heard me coming and hidden down behind them. But she couldn't keep completely still, so I heard her moving around a bit."

"But why not just come out and say hello?" asked Benny.

"Not everyone is as outgoing as you are," Violet said.

"But when we took all the stuff out of the boxcar, we didn't see her," Benny pointed out.

"She must have left when I went inside to get you guys," Violet said.

"Okay, but if she just wants to play in our

boxcar, why would she come with a flash-light in the middle of the night?" Jessie said.

"That wasn't Claire," Henry said. "The person I saw that second night was much bigger than she is."

"If that was someone else," Jessie said, "then we haven't solved the whole mystery yet."

"I'll go return Claire's book," Violet said. "Maybe she'll know something about the rest of the mystery."

"Should we all go?" asked Jessie.

"No, I think she might be more comfortable with just me," said Violet.

Picking up the book, Violet headed next door and rang the bell.

Claire answered the door.

"Hi, Claire. Is this your book?" said Violet.

Claire's face turned pink. "Yes, um, thanks."

"It was in the boxcar. It's a great place to read, isn't it?" Violet said gently.

Claire's uncomfortable look turned to a shy smile. "Yes, it is. So cozy."

"We don't mind that you were there," Violet said. "You can come over whenever you want."

Claire's face turned pink again. "I have come over before, a couple of times. . . . I wanted to play, but . . ."

"But you felt too shy to ask?" said Violet. "I've felt that way before."

"You have?" said Claire, her face brightening. Then she frowned. "I was in there when you were reading. I wanted to sneak away, but I didn't want you to think I'd been spying on you. I also ate one of your cookies. They looked so good, I just . . ."

"Couldn't resist?" said Violet with a grin. "Mrs. McGregor is a good cook. Why don't you come over now and have some more?"

Claire smiled broadly. "That would be great."

Violet had one more question. "This may sound strange, but . . . did you ever come over to the boxcar in the middle of the night?"

Claire shook her head. "Why would I do that?"

"I don't know," said Violet. "But someone has been out there, and we don't know who."

Claire said, "In the middle of the night? That's weird."

"It sure is," said Violet. "Never mind. Let's go back to my house and play."

Claire called upstairs, "Aunt Flo? I'm going over to the Aldens'."

"Okay, but don't stay too long," her aunt called back. "Your father has invited Amelia Wile to join us for dinner and she'll be here soon."

Claire turned to go, but Violet stood still.

"What's the matter?" Claire asked.

"Did your aunt say Amelia *Wile*?" Violet said.

"Yes," said Claire. "You know, the woman who is interested in boxcars?"

"Oh my goodness!" said Violet. "We have to go tell the others!"

CHAPTER 10

# All's Wile That Ends Wile

Violet ran back to the boxcar as quickly as she could, with Claire at her heels.

"Wait!" Claire called. "What's going on?"

Violet and Claire arrived breathless in the doorway of the boxcar. Jessie and Benny were sitting on the floor playing cards, and Henry was beside them, flipping through a magazine.

"You guys, you'll never believe it!" said Violet, gasping for breath.

Jessie, Benny, and Henry looked up at Violet with wonder.

*114*

"What is it?" asked Jessie.

Violet took a couple of seconds to catch her breath. "I was just over at Florence Murray's and she said that Amelia is invited to dinner."

"Um, that's nice," said Jessie, looking confused.

"You came running back to tell us *that*?" said Benny.

"She said that Amelia *Wile* is coming for dinner," Violet said.

"Amelia's last name is Wile?" said Jessie. "That means — "

"She must be related to Isabel," Henry said. "She could be her granddaughter or something."

Jessie thought a moment. "Actually, if Isabel had gotten married, her name wouldn't have been Wile anymore. So Amelia must be Louis's granddaughter — Isabel is her great aunt."

At last Claire spoke up. "What on earth are you guys talking about?"

Jessie laughed, then told Claire all about the doll and the diary they'd found.

"Amelia's grandfather must have told stories about living in a boxcar in Silver City," said Henry. "That's why she was so interested in old trains."

"She probably thought this was the boxcar where her grandfather had lived," said Violet. "That's why she kept coming back."

"Louis probably told Amelia about living in the boxcar," said Henry. "And maybe about the doll and the diary he helped his sister hide."

"Amelia did ask us if we'd ever found anything unusual here," Benny recalled.

"She might have been the one who was here at night," said Violet. "She was probably trying to find that hidden compartment."

The children heard a car door shut. "I bet that's Amelia now," said Claire, running out to see. The Aldens followed her. A small purple car was parked at the curb in front of Florence Murray's house. Amelia was walking up the front path.

"We should bring Rebecca and the diary over there," said Violet, going back into the boxcar.

"Yes," the others agreed.

Claire and the Aldens walked quickly next door. Violet was carrying the doll and the diary.

When Ms. Murray opened the door, she said, "Claire, I'm glad you're back. Amelia is here and we're going to be having dinner soon. Would you all like to join us? I can throw some more hamburgers on the grill."

"Thank you," said Henry, "but Mrs. McGregor is expecting us at home for dinner. We just wanted to show something to Amelia, if that's all right."

"Sure, come on in," said Ms. Murray.

Amelia and Professor Murray were sitting in the living room chatting. "Hello," they both said when the children entered.

"Hello," the children said.

"Amelia, we have something important to show you," said Jessie. She held out the doll and the diary.

"What's— " Amelia began, looking confused. But as soon as she opened the diary she understood. She inhaled deeply and looked as if she was about to cry.

"How did you find them?" she asked the Aldens.

"We found the doll a couple of days ago, in a hidden compartment," Henry said. "A note in its pocket told us how to find the diary."

"Isabel was your great aunt, wasn't she?" Violet asked softly.

Amelia nodded through happy tears. She turned to Professor Murray, who was looking rather puzzled.

"I never told you *why* I'm so interested in old trains," Amelia said. "My grandfather, Louis Wile, lived in a boxcar for a few months when his father lost his job. His sister, my Great Aunt Isabel, used to tell me stories about her doll and the diary she'd left there. I started to search for the boxcar they'd lived in. When I found the one in the Aldens' backyard, I knew it had to be the one. It matched everything my grandfather and great aunt had told me."

"So you came in the middle of the night to look for the doll and the diary, didn't you?" said Jessie.

Amelia nodded. "I didn't want to tell you what I was looking for. So I came at night, with my lantern."

"I thought you were a ghost!" said Benny.

"I knew you'd seen me," said Amelia. "I heard the door of your house open and I ran. I'm sorry, I think I knocked some things over."

"That's okay," said Jessie.

"You came back another time, too," said Henry.

"Yes, I did," Amelia admitted. "I parked my car at the Murrays' house and then sneaked over."

"Why didn't you just tell us the story?" Violet asked. "We would have helped you look for the doll."

Amelia shrugged. "I didn't know you, and I was afraid you might keep the doll and the diary for yourself."

Violet shook her head. "We would never do that. Those belong to you."

"We have something else for you," Jessie said. She handed Amelia the pages they'd copied from the old newspapers. Amelia's eyes opened wide as she looked at them.

"We think your great grandfather worked for that factory," Jessie explained.

Amelia nodded. "I think you're right."

"Did you find these pages at the library?" Professor Murray asked.

"Yes," said Henry.

Professor Murray smiled. "You are excellent historians."

Henry turned to Professor Murray. "We thought it might be you going in the boxcar in the middle of the night," he admitted.

"Me?" Professor Murray said. "But why?"

"We thought you wanted us to think it was haunted," said Benny.

"*Haunted?*" said Professor Murray, looking surprised.

"We thought maybe you were trying to scare us into giving up our boxcar," said Jessie.

Professor Murray smiled. "I would never do something like that. In fact, I've been rethinking what I said about your boxcar. I think you kids should keep it."

"You do?" they all said at once.

"You take very good care of that boxcar," Professor Murray said. "I've seen what a special place it is to you."

"Hooray!" shouted the Aldens.

Violet turned to Amelia. "You can come visit anytime. That boxcar is part of your family history, too."

Just then, the doorbell rang. Florence Murray went to answer it, and a moment later Mr. Alden walked into the living room.

"Grandfather!" the children shouted, running to him and nearly knocking him over with their hugs.

"When did you get home?" Jessie asked.

"Just now," Mr. Alden said. "I figured I might find you here."

"I'm so glad you're back," said Violet, hugging her grandfather again.

Mr. Alden grinned. "Did anything interesting happen while I was gone?"

"Anything interesting?" said Benny. "Just wait until you hear!"